Paul Gallico

The Snow Goose
and
The Small Miracle

Penguin Books

PENGUIN BOOKS

Published by the Penguin Group
Penguin Books Ltd, 80 Strand, London WC2R 0RL, England
Penguin Putnam Inc., 375 Hudson Street, New York, New York 10014, USA
Penguin Books Australia Ltd, 250 Camberwell Road, Camberwell, Victoria 3124, Australia
Penguin Books Canada Ltd, 10 Alcorn Avenue, Toronto, Ontario, Canada M4V 3B2
Penguin Books India (P) Ltd, 11 Community Centre, Panchsheel Park, New Delhi – 110 017, India
Penguin Books (NZ) Ltd, Cnr Rosedale and Airborne Roads, Albany, Auckland, New Zealand
Penguin Books (South Africa) (Pty) Ltd, 24 Sturdee Avenue, Rosebank 2196, South Africa

Penguin Books Ltd, Registered Offices: 80 Strand, London WC2R 0RL, England

www.penguin.com

The Snow Goose first published in the USA 1941
Published in Great Britain by Michael Joseph 1941
The Small Miracle first published by Michael Joseph 1951
Published in one volume by Penguin Books 1967

21

Printed in England by Clays Ltd, St Ives plc

ISBN-13: 978–0–140–29952–6

The Snow Goose

With drawings by Anne Linton

THE Great Marsh lies on the Essex coast between the village of Chelmbury and the ancient Saxon oyster-fishing hamlet of Wickaeldroth. It is one of the last of the wild places of England, a low, far-reaching expanse of grass and reeds and half-submerged meadowlands ending in the great saltings and mud flats and tidal pools near the restless sea.

Tidal creeks and estuaries and the crooked, meandering arms of many little rivers whose mouths lap at the edge of the ocean cut through the sodden land that seems to rise and fall and breathe with the recurrence of the daily tides. It is desolate, utterly lonely, and made lonelier by the calls and cries of the wildfowl that make their homes in the marshlands and saltings – the wildgeese and the gulls, the teal and widgeon, the redshanks and curlews that pick their way through the tidal pools. Of human habitants there are none, and none are seen, with the occasional exception of a wild-fowler or native oyster-fishermen, who still ply a trade already ancient when the Normans came to Hastings.

Greys and blues and soft greens are the colours, for when the skies are dark in the long winters, the

many waters of the beaches and marshes reflect the cold and sombre colour. But sometimes, with sunrise and sunset, sky and land are aflame with red and golden fire.

Hard by one of the winding arms of the little River Aelder runs the embankment of an old sea wall, smooth and solid, without a break, a bulwark to the land against the encroaching sea. Deep into a salting some three miles from the English Channel it runs, and there turns north. At that corner its face is gouged, broken and shattered. It has been breached, and at the breach the hungry sea has already entered and taken for its own the land, the wall, and all that stood there.

At low water the blackened and ruptured stones of the ruins of an abandoned lighthouse show above the surface, with here and there, like buoy markers, the top of a sagging fence-post. Once this lighthouse

8

abutted on the sea and was a beacon on the Essex coast. Time shifted land and water, and its usefulness came to an end.

Lately it served again as a human habitation. In it there lived a lonely man. His body was warped, but his heart was filled with love for wild and hunted things. He was ugly to look upon, but he created great beauty. It is about him, and a child who came to know him and see beyond the grotesque form that housed him to what lay within, that this story is told.

It is not a story that falls easily and smoothly into sequence. It has been garnered from many sources and from many people. Some of it comes in the form of fragments from men who looked upon strange and violent scenes. For the sea has claimed its own and spreads its rippled blanket over the site, and the great white bird with the black-tipped pinions that saw it all from the beginning to the end has returned to the dark, frozen silences of the northlands whence it came.

I N the late spring of 1930 Philip Rhayader came to the abandoned lighthouse at the mouth of the Aelder. He bought the light and many acres of marshland and salting surrounding it.

He lived and worked there alone the year round. He was a painter of birds and of nature, who, for reasons, had withdrawn from all human society. Some of the reasons were apparent on his fortnightly visits to the little village of Chelmbury for supplies, where the natives looked askance at his mis-shapen body and dark visage. For he was a hunchback and his left arm was crippled, thin and bent at the wrist, like the claw of a bird.

They soon became used to his queer figure, small but powerful, the massive, dark, bearded head set just slightly below the mysterious mound on his back, the glowing eyes and the clawed hand, and marked him off as 'that queer painter chap that lives down to lighthouse.'

Physical deformity often breeds hatred of human-ity in men. Rhayader did not hate; he loved very greatly, man, the animal kingdom, and all nature.

His heart was filled with pity and understanding. He had mastered his handicap, but he could not master the rebuffs he suffered, due to his appearance. The thing that drove him into seclusion was his failure to find anywhere a return of the warmth that flowed from him. He repelled women. Men would have warmed to him had they got to know him. But the mere fact that an effort was being made hurt Rhayader and drove him to avoid the person making it.

He was twenty-seven when he came to the Great Marsh. He had travelled much and fought valiantly before he made the decision to withdraw from a world in which he could not take part as other men. For all the artist's sensitivity and woman's tenderness locked in his barrel breast, he was very much a man.

In his retreat he had his birds, his paintings, and his boat. He owned a sixteen-footer, which he sailed with wonderful skill. Alone, with no eyes to watch him, he managed well with his deformed hand, and he often used his strong teeth to handle the sheets of his billowing sails in a tricky blow.

He would sail the tidal creek and estuaries and out to sea, and would be gone for days at a time, looking for new species of birds to photograph or sketch, and he became an adept at netting them to add to his collection of tamed wildfowl in the pen

near his studio that formed the nucleus of a sanctuary.

He never shot over a bird, and wild-fowlers were not welcome near his premises. He was a friend to all things wild, and the wild things repaid him with their friendship.

Tamed in his enclosures were the geese that came winging down the coast from Iceland and Spitzbergen each October, in great skeins that darkened the sky and filled the air with the rushing noise of their passage – the brown-bodied pink-feet, white-breasted barnacles, with their dark necks and clowns' masks,

the wild white fronts with black-barred breasts, and many species of wild ducks – widgeon, mallard, pintails, teal and shovellers.

Some were pinioned, so that they would remain there as a sign and signal to the wild ones that came down at each winter's beginning that here were food and sanctuary.

Many hundreds came and remained with him all through the cold weather from October to the early spring, when they migrated north again to their breeding-grounds below the ice rim.

Rhayader was content in the knowledge that when storms blew, or it was bitter cold and food was scarce, or the big punt guns of the distant bag hunters roared, his birds were safe; that he had gathered to the sanctuary and security of his own arms and heart these many wild and beautiful creatures who knew and trusted him.

They would answer the call of the north in the spring, but in the fall they would come back, barking and whooping and honking in the autumn sky, to circle the landmark of the old light and drop to earth near by to be his guests again – birds that he well remembered and recognized from the previous year.

And this made Rhayader happy, because he knew that implanted somewhere in their beings was the germ knowledge of his existence and his safe haven, that this knowledge had become a part of them and, with the coming of the grey skies and the winds from the north, would send them unerringly back to him.

For the rest, his heart and soul went into the painting of the country in which he lived and its creatures. There are not many Rhayaders extant. He hoarded them jealously, piling them up in his lighthouse and the storerooms above by the hundreds. He was not satisfied with them, because as an artist he was uncompromising.

But the few that have reached the market are masterpieces, filled with the glow and colours of marsh-reflected light, the feel of flight, the push of birds breasting a morning wind bending the tall flag reeds. He painted the loneliness and the smell of the salt-laden cold, the eternity and agelessness of marshes, the wild, living creatures, dawn flights, and frightened things taking to the air, and winged shadows at night hiding from the moon.

ONE November afternoon, three years after Rhayader had come to the Great Marsh, a child approached the lighthouse studio by means of the sea wall. In her arms she carried a burden.

She was no more than twelve, slender, dirty, nervous and timid as a bird, but beneath the grime as eerily beautiful as a marsh faery. She was pure Saxon, large-boned, fair, with a head to which her body was yet to grow, and deep-set, violet-coloured eyes.

She was desperately frightened of the ugly man she had come to see, for legend had already begun to gather about Rhayader, and the native wild-fowlers hated him for interfering with their sport.

But greater than her fear was the need of that which she bore. For locked in her child's heart was the knowledge, picked up somewhere in the swampland, that this ogre who lived in the lighthouse had magic that could heal injured things.

She had never seen Rhayader before and was close to fleeing in panic at the dark apparition that appeared at the studio door, drawn by her footsteps

– the black head and beard, the sinister hump, and the crooked claw.

She stood there staring, poised like a disturbed marsh bird for instant flight.

But his voice was deep and kind when he spoke to her.

'What is it, child?'

She stood her ground, and then edged timidly forward. The thing she carried in her arms was a large white bird, and it was quite still. There were stains of blood on its whiteness and on her kirtle where she had held it to her.

The girl placed it in his arms. 'I found it, sir. It's hurted. Is it still alive?'

'Yes. Yes, I think so. Come in, child, come in.'

Rhayader went inside, bearing the bird, which he placed upon a table, where it moved feebly. Curiosity overcame fear. The girl followed and found herself in a room warmed by a coal fire, shining with many coloured pictures that covered the walls, and full of a strange but pleasant smell.

The bird fluttered. With his good hand Rhayader spread one of its immense white pinions. The end was beautifully tipped with black.

Rhayader looked and marvelled, and said: 'Child: where did you find it?'

'In t' marsh, sir, where fowlers had been. What – what is it, sir?'

'It's a snow goose from Canada. But how in all heaven came it here?'

The name seemed to mean nothing to the little girl. Her deep violet eyes, shining out of the dirt on her thin face, were fixed with concern on the injured bird.

She said: 'Can 'ee heal it, sir?'

'Yes, yes,' said Rhayader. 'We will try. Come, you shall help me.'

There were scissors and bandages and splints on a shelf, and he was marvellously deft, even with the crooked claw that managed to hold things.

He said: 'Ah, she has been shot, poor thing. Her leg is broken, and the wing tip! but not badly. See, we will clip her primaries, so that we can bandage it, but in the spring the feathers will grow and she will be able to fly again. We'll bandage it close to her body, so that she cannot move it until it has set, and then make a splint for the poor leg.'

Her fears forgotten, the child watched, fascinated, as he worked, and all the more so because while he fixed a fine splint to the shattered leg he told her the most wonderful story.

The bird was a young one, no more than a year old. She was born in a northern land far, far across the seas, a land belonging to England. Flying to the south to escape the snow and ice and bitter cold, a great storm had seized her and whirled and buffeted her about. It was a truly terrible storm, stronger than her great wings, stronger than anything. For days and nights it held her in its grip and there was nothing she could do but fly before it. When finally it had blown itself out and her sure instincts took her south again, she was over a different land and surrounded by strange birds that she had never seen before. At last, exhausted by her ordeal, she had sunk to rest in a friendly green marsh, only to be met by the blast from the hunter's gun.

'A bitter reception for a visiting princess,' concluded Rhayader. 'We will call her "*La Princesse Perdue*," the Lost Princess. And in a few days she will be feeling much better. See!' He reached into his pocket and produced a handful of grain. The snow goose opened its round yellow eyes and nibbled at it.

The child laughed with delight, and then suddenly caught her breath with alarm as the full import of where she was pressed in upon her, and without a word she turned and fled out of the door.

'Wait, wait!' cried Rhayader, and went to the entrance, where he stopped so that it framed his dark bulk. The girl was already fleeing down the sea wall, but she paused at his voice and looked back.

'What is your name, child?'

'Frith.'

'Eh?' said Rhayader. 'Fritha, I suppose. Where do you live?'

'Wi' t' fisherfolk at Wickaeldroth.' She gave the name the old Saxon pronunciation.

'Will you come back tomorrow, or the next day, to see how the Princess is getting along?'

She paused, and again Rhayader must have thought of the wild water birds caught motionless in that split second of alarm before they took to flight.

But her thin voice came back to him: 'Ay!'

And then she was gone, with her fair hair streaming out behind her.

The snow goose mended rapidly and by midwinter was already limping about the enclosure with the wild pink-footed geese with which it associated, rather than the barnacles, and had learned to come to be fed at Rhayader's call. And the child, Fritha, or Frith, was a frequent visitor. She had overcome her fear of Rhayader. Her imagination was captured by the presence of this strange white princess from a land far over the sea, a land that was all pink, as she knew from the map that Rhayader showed her, and on which they traced the stormy path of the lost bird from its home in Canada to the Great Marsh of Essex.

Then one June morning a group of late pink-feet, fat and well fed from the winter at the lighthouse, answered the stronger call of the breeding-grounds and rose lazily, climbing into the sky in ever widening circles. With them, her white body and black-tipped pinions shining in the spring sun, was the snow goose. It so happened that Frith was at the light-house. Her cry brought Rhayader running from the studio.

'Look! Look! The Princess! Be she going away?'

Rhayader stared into the sky at the climbing specks. 'Ay,' he said, unconsciously dropping into her manner of speech. 'The Princess is going home. Listen! she is bidding us farewell.'

Out of the clear sky came the mournful barking of the pink-feet, and above it the higher, clearer note of the snow goose. The specks drifted northward, formed into a tiny v, diminished, and vanished.

With the departure of the snow goose ended the visits of Frith to the lighthouse. Rhayader learned all over again the meaning of the word 'loneliness'.

That summer, out of his memory, he painted a picture of a slender, grime-covered child, her fair hair blown by a November storm, who bore in her arms a wounded white bird.

IN mid-October the miracle occurred. Rhayader was in his enclosure, feeding his birds. A grey north-east wind was blowing and the land was sighing beneath the incoming tide. Above the sea and the wind noises he heard a clear, high note. He turned his eyes upward to the evening sky in time to see first an infinite speck, then a black-and-white pinioned dream that circled the lighthouse once, and finally a reality that dropped to earth in the pen and came waddling forward importantly to be fed, as though she had never been away. It was the snow goose. There was no mistaking her. Tears of joy came to Rhayader's eyes. Where had she been? Surely not home to Canada. No, she must have summered in Greenland or Spitzbergen with the pink-feet. She had remembered and had returned.

When next Rhayader went into Chelmbury for supplies, he left a message with the postmistress – one that must have caused her much bewilderment. He said: 'Tell Frith, who lives with the fisherfolk at Wickaeldroth, that the Lost Princess has returned.'

Three days later, Frith, taller, still tousled and

unkempt, came shyly to the lighthouse to visit *La Princesse Perdue*.

Time passed. On the Great Marsh it was marked by the height of the tides, the slow march of the seasons, the passage of the birds, and, for Rhayader, by the arrival and departure of the snow goose.

The world outside boiled and seethed and rumbled with the eruption that was soon to break forth and come close to marking its destruction. But not yet did it touch upon Rhayader, or, for that matter, Frith. They had fallen into a curious natural rhythm, even as the child grew older. When the snow goose was at the lighthouse, then she came, too, to visit and learn many things from Rhayader. They sailed together in his speedy boat, that he handled so skilfully. They caught wildfowl for the ever-increasing colony, and built new pens and enclosures for them. From him she learned the lore of every wild bird, from gull to gyrfalcon, that flew the marshes. She cooked for him sometimes, and even learned to mix his paints.

But when the snow goose returned to its summer home it was as though some kind of bar was up between them, and she did not come to the lighthouse. One year the bird did not return, and Rhayader was heartbroken. All things seemed to have ended for him. He painted furiously through the winter and the next summer, and never once saw the child. But in the fall the familiar cry once more rang from the sky, and the huge white bird, now at its full growth, dropped from the skies as mysteriously as it had departed. Joyously, Rhayader sailed his boat into Chelmbury and left his message with the postmistress

Curiously, it was more than a month after he had left the message before Frith reappeared at the lighthouse, and Rhayader, with a shock, realized that she was a child no longer.

After the year in which the bird had remained away, its periods of absence grew shorter and shorter. It grew so tame that it followed Rhayader about and even came into the studio while he was working.

IN the spring of 1940 the birds migrated early from the Great Marsh. The world was on fire. The whine and roar of the bombers and the thudding explosions frightened them. The first day of May, Frith and Rhayader stood shoulder to shoulder on the sea wall and watched the last of the unpinioned pink-feet and barnacle geese rise from their sanctuary; she, tall, slender, free as air and hauntingly beautiful; he, dark, grotesque, his massive bearded head raised to the sky, his glowing dark eyes watching the geese form their flight tracery.

'Look, Philip,' Frith said.

Rhayader followed her eyes. The snow goose had taken flight, her giant wings spread, but she was flying low, and once came quite close to them, so that for a moment the spreading black-tipped, white pinions seemed to caress them and they felt the rush of the bird's swift passage. Once, twice, she circled the lighthouse, then dropped to earth again in the enclosure with the pinioned geese and commenced to feed.

'She be'ent going,' said Frith, with marvel in her voice. The bird in its close passage seemed to have woven a kind of magic about her. 'The Princess be goin' t' stay.'

'Ay,' said Rhayader, and his voice was shaken too. 'She'll stay. She will never go away again. The Lost Princess is lost no more. This is her home now – of her own free will.'

The spell the bird had girt about her was broken, and Frith was suddenly conscious of the fact that she was frightened, and the things that frightened her were in Rhayader's eyes – the longing and the loneliness and the deep, welling, unspoken things that lay in and behind them as he turned them upon her.

His last words were repeating themselves in her head as though he had said them again: 'This is her home now – of her own free will.' The delicate tendrils of her instincts reached to him and carried to her the message of the things he could not speak because of what he felt himself to be, mis-shapen and grotesque. And where his voice might have soothed her, her fright grew greater at his silence and the power of the unspoken things between them. The woman in her bade her take flight from something that she was not yet capable of understanding.

Frith said: 'I – I must go. Good-bye. I be glad the – the Princess will stay. You'll not be so alone now.'

She turned and walked swiftly away, and his sadly spoken 'Good-bye, Frith,' was only a half-heard ghost of a sound borne to her ears above the rustling of the marsh grass. She was far away before she dared turn for a backward glance. He was still standing on the sea wall, a dark speck against the sky.

Her fear had stilled now. It had been replaced by something else, a queer sense of loss that made her stand quite still for a moment, so sharp was it. Then, more slowly, she continued on, away from the sky-ward-pointing finger of the lighthouse and the man beneath it.

I T was a little more than three weeks before F
returned to the lighthouse. May was at its end,
the day, too, in a long golden twilight that was giv
way to the silver of the moon already hanging in
eastern sky.

She told herself, as her steps took her thither, t
she must know whether the snow goose had rea
stayed, as Rhayader said it would. Perhaps it h
flown away, after all. But her firm tread on the s
wall was full of eagerness and sometimes unconsciously she found herself hurrying.

Frith saw the yellow light of Rhayader's lantern
down by his little wharf, and she found him there.
His sailboat was rocking gently on a flooding tide and
he was loading supplies into her – water and foo
and bottles of brandy, gear and a spare sail. Wh
he turned to the sound of her coming, she saw t
he was pale, but that his dark eyes, usually so
and placid, were glowing with excitement, an
was breathing heavily from his exertions.

Sudden alarm seized Frith. The snow goo
forgotten. 'Philip! Ye be goin' away?'

Rhayader paused in his work to greet 1

there was something in his face, a glow and a look, that she had never seen there before.

'Frith! I am glad you came. Yes, I must go away. A little trip. I will come back.' His usually kindly voice was hoarse with what was suppressed inside him.

Frith asked: 'Where must ye go?'

Words came tumbling from Rhayader now. He must go to Dunkirk. A hundred miles across the Channel. A British army was trapped there on the sands, awaiting destruction at the hands of the advancing Germans. The port was in flames, the position hopeless. He had heard it in the village when he had gone for supplies. Men were putting out from Chelmbury in answer to the government's call, every tug and fishing boat or power launch that could propel itself was heading across the Channel to haul the men off the beaches to the transports and destroyers that could not reach the shallows, to rescue as many as possible from the Germans' fire.

Frith listened and felt her heart dying within her. He was saying that he would sail the Channel in his little boat. It could take six men at a time; in a pinch, seven. He could make many trips from the beaches to the transports.

The girl was young, primitive, inarticulate. She did not understand war, or what had happened in France, or the meaning of the trapped army, but the blood witnin her told her that here was danger.

'Philip! Must 'ee go? You'll not come back. Why must it be 'ee?'

The fever seemed to have gone from Rhayader's soul with the first rush of words, and he explained it to her in terms that she could understand.

He said: 'Men are huddled on the beaches like hunted birds, Frith, like the wounded and hunted birds we used to find and bring to sanctuary. Over them fly the steel peregrines, hawks, and gyrfalcons, and they have no shelter from these iron birds of prey. They are lost and storm-driven and harried, like the *Princesse Perdue* you found and brought to me out of the marshes many years ago, and we healed her. They need help, my dear, as our wild creatures have needed help, and that is why I must go. It is something that I can do. Yes, I can. For once – for once I can be a man and play my part.'

Frith stared at Rhayader. He had changed so. For the first time she saw that he was no longer ugly or mis-shapen or grotesque, but very beautiful. Things were turmoiling in her own soul, crying to be said, and she did not know how to say them.

'I'll come with 'ee! Philip.'

Rhayader shook his head. 'Your place in the boat would cause a soldier to be left behind, and another, and another. I must go alone.'

He donned rubber coat and boots and took to his boat. He waved and called back: 'Good-bye! Will you look after the birds until I return, Frith?'

Frith's hand came up, but only half, to wave too. 'God speed you,' she said, but gave it the Saxon turn. 'I will take care of t' birds. God-speed, Philip.'

It was night now, bright with moon fragment and

stars and northern glow. Frith stood on the sea wall and watched the sail gliding down the swollen estuary. Suddenly from the darkness behind her there came a rush of wings, and something swept past her into the air. In the night light she saw the flash of white wings, black-tipped, and the thrust-forward head of the snow goose.

It rose and cruised over the lighthouse once and then headed down the winding creek where Rhayader's sail was slanting in the gaining breeze, and flew above him in slow, wide circles.

White sail and white bird were visible for a long time.

'Watch o'er him. Watch o'er him,' Frith whispered. When they were both out of sight at last, she turned and walked slowly, with bent head, back to the empty lighthouse.

Now the story becomes fragmentary, and one of these fragments is in the words of the men on leave who told it in the public room of the Crown and Arrow, an East Chapel pub.

'A goose, a bloomin' goose, so 'elp me,' said Private Potton, of His Majesty's London Rifles.

'Garn,' said a bandy-legged artilleryman.

'A goose it was. Jock, 'ere, seed it same as me. It come flyin' down outa the muck an' stink an' smoke of Dunkirk that was over'ead. It was white, wiv black on its wings, an' it circles us like a bloomin' dive bomber. Jock, 'ere, 'e sez: "We're done for. It's the hangel of death a-come for us."

'"Garn," Hi sez, "it's a ruddy goose, come over from 'ome wiv a message from Churchill, an' 'ow are we henjoying the bloomin' bathing. It's a omen, that's what it is, a bloody omen. We'll get out of this yet, me lad."

'We was roostin' on the beach between Dunkirk an' Lapanny, like a lot o' bloomin' pigeons on Victoria Hembankment, waitin' for Jerry to pot us. 'E potted us good too. 'E was be'ind us an' flankin' us an' above us. 'E give us shrapnel and 'e give us H.E.,

an' 'e peppers us from the bloomin' hatmosphere
with Jittersmiths.

'An' offshore is the *Kentish Maid*, a ruddy hex-
cursion scow wot Hi've taken many a trip on out of
Margate in the summer, for two-and-six, waiting to
take us off, 'arf a mile out from the bloomin' shallows.

'While we are lyin' there on the beach, done in an'
cursin' becos there ain't no way to get out to the
boat, a Stuka dives on 'er, an' 'is bombs drop along-
side of 'er, throwin' up water like the bloomin' foun-
tains in the palace gardens; a reg'lar display it was.

'Then a destroyer come up an' says: "No, ye
don't" to the Stuka with ack-acks and pom-poms,
but another Jerry dives on the destroyer, an' 'its 'er.
Coo, did she go up! She burned before she sunk, an'
the smoke an' the stink come driftin' inshore, all yellow an' black, an' out of it comes this bloomin' goose,
a-circlin' around us trapped on the beach.

'An' then around a bend 'e comes in a bloody little
sailboat, sailing along as cool as you please, like a
bloomin' toff out for a pleasure spin on a Sunday
hafternoon at 'Enley.'

''Oo comes?' inquired a civilian.

''Im! 'Im that saved a lot of us. 'E sailed clean
through a boil of machine-gun bullets from a Jerry
in a Jittersmith wot was strafin' – a Ramsgate motorboat wot 'ad tried to take us off 'ad been sunk there

'arf an hour ago – the water was all frothin' with shell splashes an' bullets, but 'e didn't give it no mind, 'e didn't. 'E didn't 'ave no petrol to burn or hexplode, an' he sailed in between the shells.

'Into the shallows 'e come out of the black smoke of the burnin' destroyer, a little dark man wiv a beard, a bloomin' claw for a 'and, an' a 'ump on 'is back.

    ''E 'ad a rope in 'is teeth that was shinin' white out of 'is black beard, 'is good 'and on the tiller an' the crooked one beckonin' to us to come. An' over'ead, around and around, flied the ruddy goose.

    'Jock, 'ere, says: "Lawk, it's all over now. It's the bloody devil come for us 'imself. Hi must 'ave been struck an' don't know it."

    ' "Garn," I sez, "it's more like the good Lord, 'e looks to me, than any bloomin' devil." 'E did, too, like the pictures from the Sunday-school books, wiv 'is white face and dark eyes an' beard an' all, and 'is bloomin' boat.

'"Hi can taken seven at a time," 'e sings out when 'e's in close.

'Our horfficer shouts: "Good man! . . . You seven nearest, get in."

'We waded out to where 'e was. Hi was that weary Hi couldn't climb over the side, but 'e takes me by the collar of me tunic an' pulls, wiv a "In ye go, lad. Come on. Next man."

'An' in Hi went. Coo, 'e was strong, 'e was. Then 'e sets 'is sail, part of wot looks like a bloomin' sieve from machine-gun bullets, shouts: "Keep down in the bottom of the boat, boys, in case we meet any of yer friends," and we're off, 'im sittin' in the stern wiv 'is rope in 'is teeth, another in 'is crooked claw, an' 'is right 'and on the tiller, a-steerin' an' sailin' through the spray of the shells thrown by a land battery somewhere back of the coast. An' the bloomin' goose is flyin' around and around, 'onking above the wind and the row Jerry was makin', like a bloomin' Morris on Winchester by-pass.

'"Hi told you yon goose was a omen," Hi sez to Jock. "Look at 'im there, a bloomin' hangel of mercy."

''Im at the tiller just looks up at the goose, wiv the rope in 'is teeth, an' grins at 'er like 'e knows 'er a lifetime.

''E brung us out to the *Kentish Maid* and turns around and goes back for another load. 'E made trips all afternoon an' all night, too, because the bloody light of Dunkirk burning was bright enough to see by. Hi don't know 'ow many trips 'e made, but 'im an' a nobby Thames Yacht Club motorboat an' a big lifeboat from Poole that come along brought off all there was of us on that particular stretch of hell, without the loss of a man.

'We sailed when the last man was off, an' there was more than seven hunder' of us haboard a boat built to take two hunder'. 'E was still there when we left, an' 'e waved us good-bye and sails off towards Dunkirk, and the bird wiv 'im. Blimy, it was queer to see that ruddy big goose flyin' around 'is boat, lit up by the fires like a white hangel against the smoke.

'A Stuka 'ad another go at us, 'arfway across, but 'e'd been stayin' up late nights, an' missed. By mornin' we was safe 'ome.

'Hi never did find out what become of 'im, or 'oo 'e was – 'im wiv the 'ump an' 'is little sail-boat. A bloody good man 'e was, that chap.'

'Coo,' said the artilleryman. 'A ruddy big goose. Whatcher know?'

IN an officer's club in Brook Street, a retired naval officer, sixty-five years old, Commander Keith Brill-Oudener, was telling of his experiences during the evacuation of Dunkirk. Called out of bed at four o'clock in the morning, he had captained a lopsided Limehouse tug across the Channel, towing a string of Thames barges, which he brought back four times loaded with soldiers. On his last trip he came in with her funnel shot away and a hole in her side. But he got her back to Dover.

A naval-reserve officer, who had two Brixham trawlers and a Yarmouth drifter blasted out from under him in the last four days of the evacuation, said: 'Did you run across that queer sort of legend about a wild goose? It was all up and down the beaches. You know how those things spring up. Some of the men I brought back were talking about it. It was supposed to have appeared at intervals the last days between Dunkirk and La Panne. If you saw it, you were eventually saved. That sort of thing.'

'H'm'm'm,' said Brill-Oudener, 'a wild goose. I saw a tame one. Dashed strange experience. Tragic in a way, too. And lucky for us. Tell you about it. Third trip back. Toward six o'clock we sighted a derelict small boat. Seemed to be a chap or a body in her. And a bird perched on the rail.

'We changed our course when we got nearer, and went over for a look-see. By Gad, it was a chap. Or had been, poor fellow. Machine-gunned, you know. Badly. Face down in the water. Bird was a goose, a tame one.

'We drifted close, but when one of our chaps reached over, the bird hissed at him and struck at him with her wings. Couldn't drive it off. Suddenly young Kettering, who was with me, gave a hail and pointed to starboard. Big mine floating by. One of Jerry's beauties. If we'd kept on our course we'd have piled right into it. Ugh! Head on. We let it get a hundred yards astern of the last barge, and the men blew it up with rifle-fire.

'When we turned our attention to the derelict again, she was gone. Sunk. Concussion, you know. Chap with her. He must have been lashed to her. The bird had got up and was circling. Three times, like a plane saluting. Dashed queer feeling. Then she flew off to the west. Lucky thing for us we went over to have a look, eh? Odd that you should mention a goose.'

FRITHA remained alone at the little lighthouse on the Great Marsh, taking care of the pinioned birds, waiting for she knew not what. The first days she haunted the sea wall, watching; though she knew it was useless. Later she roamed through the store-rooms of the lighthouse building with their stacks of canvases on which Rhayader had captured every mood and light of the desolate country and the wondrous, graceful, feathered things that inhabited it.

Among them she found the picture that Rhayader had painted of her from memory so many years ago, when she was still a child, and had stood, wind-blown and timid, at his threshold, hugging an injured bird to her.

The picture and the things she saw in it stirred her as nothing ever had before, for much of Rhayader's soul had gone into it. Strangely, it was the only time he had painted the snow goose, the lost wild creature, storm-driven from another land, that to each had brought a friend, and which, in the end, returned to her with the message that she would never see him again.

Long before the snow goose had come dropping

out of a crimsoned eastern sky to circle the light-house in a last farewell, Fritha, from the ancient powers of the blood that was in her, knew that Rhayader would not return.

And so, when one sunset she heard the high-pitched, well-remembered note cried from the heavens, it brought no instant of false hope to her heart. This moment, it seemed, she had lived before many times.

She came running to the sea wall and turned her eyes, not toward the distant Channel whence a sail might come, but in the sky from whose flaming arches plummeted the snow goose. Then the sight, the sound, and the solitude surrounding broke the dam within her and released the surging, overwhelming truth of her love, let it well forth in tears.

Wild spirit called to wild spirit, and she seemed to be flying with the great bird, soaring with it in the evening sky and hearkening to Rhayader's message.

Sky and earth were trembling with it and filled her beyond the bearing of it. 'Frith! Fritha! Frith, my love. Good-bye, my love.' The white pinions, black-tipped, were beating it out upon her heart, and her heart was answering: 'Philip, I love 'ee.'

For a moment Frith thought the snow goose was going to land in the old enclosure, as the pinioned geese set up a welcoming gabble. But it only skimmed low, then soared up again, flew in a wide, graceful spiral once around the old light, and then began to climb.

Watching it, Frith saw no longer the snow goose but the soul of Rhayader taking farewell of her before departing for ever.

She was no longer flying with it! but earth-bound. She stretched her arms up into the sky and stood on tip-toes, reaching, and cried: 'God-speed, God-speed, Philip!'

Frith's tears were stilled. She stood watching silently long after the goose had vanished. Then she went into the lighthouse and secured the picture that Rhayader had painted of her. Hugging it to her breast, she wended her way homeward along the old sea wall.

EACH night, for many weeks thereafter, Frith came to the lighthouse and fed the pinioned birds. Then one early morning a German pilot on a dawn raid mistook the old abandoned light for an active military objective, dived on to it, a screaming steel hawk, and blew it and all it contained into oblivion.

That evening when Fritha came, the sea had moved in through the breached walls and covered it over. Nothing was left to break the utter desolation. No marsh fowl had dared to return. Only the frightless gulls wheeled and soared and mewed their plaint over the place where it had been.

The Small Miracle

With drawings by Edgar Norfield

To St Francis
a man among saints

APPROACHING Assisi via the chalky, dusty road that twists its way up Monte Subasio, now revealing, now concealing the exquisite little town, as it winds its way through olive and cypress groves, you eventually reach a division where your choice lies between an upper and a lower route.

If you select the latter, you soon find yourself entering Assisi through the twelfth-century archway of the denticulated door of St Francis. But if, seduced by the clear air, the wish to mount even closer to the canopy of blue Italian sky and expose still more of the delectable view of the rich Umbrian valley below, you choose the upper way, you and your vehicle eventually become inextricably entangled in the welter of humanity, oxen, goats, bawling calves, mules, fowl, children, pigs, booths and carts gathered at the market place outside the walls.

It is here you would be most likely to encounter Pepino, with his donkey Violetta, hard at work, turning his hand to anything whereby a small boy and a strong, willing beast of burden could win for themselves the crumpled ten and twenty lira notes needed to buy food and pay for lodging in the barn of Niccolo the stableman.

Pepino and Violetta were everything to each other. They were a familiar sight about Assisi and its immediate environs – the thin brown boy, ragged and barefooted, with the enormous dark eyes, large ears, and close-cropped, upstanding hair, and the dust-coloured little donkey with the Mona Lisa smile.

Pepino was ten years old and an orphan, his father, mother and near relatives having been killed in the war. In self-reliance, wisdom and demeanour he was, of course, much older, a circumstance aided by his independence, for Pepino was an unusual orphan in that having a heritage he need rely on no one. Pepino's heritage was Violetta.

She was a good, useful and docile donkey, alike as any other with friendly, gentle eyes, soft taupe-coloured muzzle, and long, pointed brown ears, with one exception that distinguished her. Violetta had a curious expression about the corners of her mouth, as though she were smiling gently over something that amused or pleased her. Thus, no matter what kind of work, or how much she was asked to do, she always appeared to be performing it with a smile of quiet satisfaction. The combination of Pepino's dark lustrous eyes and Violetta's smile was so harmonious that people favoured them and they were able not only to earn enough for their keep but, aided and

advised by Father Damico, the priest of their parish, to save a little as well.

There were all kinds of things they could do – carry loads of wood or water, deliver purchases carried in the panniers that thumped against Violetta's sides, hire out to help pull a cart mired in the mud, aid in the olive harvest, and even, occasionally, help some citizen who was too encumbered with wine to reach his home on foot, by means of a four-footed taxi with Pepino walking beside to see that the drunkard did not fall off.

But this was not the only reason for the love that existed between boy and donkey, for Violetta was more than just the means of his livelihood. She was mother to him, and father, brother, playmate, companion, and comfort. At night, in the straw of Niccolo's stable, Pepino slept curled up close to her when it was cold, his head pillowed on her neck.

Since the mountainside was a rough world for a small boy, he was sometimes beaten or injured, and then he could creep to her for comfort and Violetta would gently nuzzle his bruises. When there was joy in his heart, he shouted songs into her waving ears; when he was lonely and hurt, he could lean his head against her soft, warm flank and cry out his tears.

On his part, he fed her, watered her, searched her for ticks and parasites, picked stones from her hoofs, scratched and groomed and curried her, lavished affection on her, particularly when they were alone, while in public he never beat her with the donkey stick more than was necessary. For this treatment Violetta made a god of Pepino, and repaid him with loyalty, obedience and affection.

Thus, when one day in the early spring Violetta fell ill, it was the most serious thing that had ever happened to Pepino. It began first with an unusual lethargy that would respond neither to stick nor caresses, nor the young, strident voice urging her on. Later Pepino observed other symptoms and a visible loss of weight. Her ribs, once so well padded, began to show through her sides. But most distressing, either through a change in the conformation of her head, due to growing thinner, or because of the distress of the illness, Violetta lost her enchanting and lovable smile.

Drawing upon his carefully hoarded reserves of lira notes and parting with several of the impressive denomination of a hundred, Pepino called in Dr Bartoli, the vet.

The vet. examined her in good faith, dosed her, and tried his best; but she did not improve and, instead, continued to lose weight and grow weaker. He hummed and hawed then and said, 'Well, now, it is hard to say. It might be one thing, such as the bite of a fly new to this district, or another, such as a germ settling in the intestine.' Either way, how could

one tell? There had been a similar case in Foligno and another in a far-away town. He recommended resting the beast and feeding her lightly. If the illness passed from her and God willed, she might live. Otherwise, she would surely die and there would be an end to her suffering.

After he had gone away, Pepino put his cropped head on Violetta's heaving flank and wept unrestrainedly. But then, when the storm, induced by the fear of losing his only companion in the world, had subsided, he knew what he must do. If there was no help for Violetta on earth, the appeal must be registered above. His plan was nothing less than to take Violetta into the crypt beneath the lower church of the Basilica of St Francis, where rested the remains of the Saint who had so dearly loved God's creations, including all the feathered and the four-footed brothers and sisters who served Him. There he would beg St Francis to heal her. Pepino had no doubt that the Saint would do so when he saw Violetta.

These things Pepino knew from Father Damico, who had a way of talking about St Francis as though he were a living person who might still be encountered in his frayed cowl, bound with a hemp cord at the middle, merely by turning a corner of the Main Square in Assisi or by walking down one of the narrow, cobbled streets.

And besides, there was a precedent. Giani, his friend, the son of Niccolo the stableman, had taken his sick kitten into the crypt and asked St Francis to heal her, and the cat had got well – at least half well, anyway, for her hind legs still dragged a little; but at least she had not died. Pepino felt that if Violetta were to die, it would be the end of everything for him.

Thereupon, with considerable difficulty, he persuaded the sick and shaky donkey to rise, and with urgings and caresses and minimum use of the stick drove her through the crooked streets of Assisi and up the hill to the Basilica of St Francis. At the beautiful twin portal of the lower church he respectfully asked Fra Bernard, who was on duty there, for permission to take Violetta down to St Francis, so that she might be made well again.

Fra Bernard was a new monk, and, calling Pepino a young and impious scoundrel, ordered him and his donkey to be off. It was strictly forbidden to bring livestock into the church, and even to think of taking an ass into the crypt of St Francis was a desecration. And besides, how did he imagine she would get down there when the narrow, winding staircase was barely wide enough to accommodate humans in single file, much less four-footed animals? Pepino must be a fool as well as a shiftless rascal.

As ordered, Pepino retreated from the portal, his arm about Violetta's neck, and bethought himself of what he must do next to succeed in his purpose, for while he was disappointed at the rebuff he had received, he was not at all discouraged.

Despite the tragedy that had struck Pepino's early life and robbed him of his family, he really considered himself a most fortunate boy, compared with many, since he had acquired not only a heritage to aid him in earning a living but also an important precept by which to live.

This maxim, the golden key to success, had been left with Pepino, together with bars of chocolate, chewing gum, peanut brittle, soap, and other delights, by a corporal in the United States Army who had, in the six months he had been stationed in the vicinity of Assisi, been Pepino's demigod and hero. His name was Francis Xavier O'Halloran, and what he told Pepino before he departed out of his life for ever was, 'If you want to get ahead in this world, kid, don't never take no for an answer. Get it?' Pepino never forgot this important advice.

He thought now that his next step was clear; nevertheless, he went first to his friend and adviser, Father Damico, for confirmation.

Father Damico, who had a broad head, lustrous eyes, and shoulders shaped as though they had been especially designed to support the burdens laid upon them by his parishioners, said, 'You are within your rights, my son, in taking your request to the lay Supervisor and it lies within his power to grant or refuse it.'

There was no malice in the encouragement he thus gave Pepino, but it was also true that he was not loath to see the Supervisor brought face to face with

an example of pure and innocent faith. For in his private opinion that worthy man was too much concerned with the twin churches that formed the Basilica and the crypt as a tourist attraction. He, Father Damico, could not see why the child should not have his wish, but, of course, it was out of his jurisdiction. He was, however, curious about how the Supervisor would react, even though he thought he knew in advance.

However, he did not impart his fears to Pepino and merely called after him as he was leaving, 'And if the little one cannot be got in from above, there is another entrance from below, through the old church, only it has been walled up for a hundred years. But it could be opened. You might remind the Supervisor when you see him. He knows where it is.'

Pepino thanked him and went back alone to the Basilica and the monastery attached to it and asked permission to see the Supervisor.

This personage was an accessible man, and even though he was engaged in a conversation with the Bishop, he sent for Pepino, who walked into the cloister gardens where he waited respectfully for the two great men to finish.

The two dignitaries were walking up and down, and Pepino wished it were the Bishop who was to say yea or nay to his request, as he looked the kindlier of the two, the Supervisor appearing to have more the expression of a merchant. The boy pricked up his ears, because, as it happened, so they were speaking of St Francis, and the Bishop was just remarking with a sigh, 'He has been gone too long from this earth. The lesson of his life is plain to all who can read. But who in these times will pause to do so?'

The Supervisor said, 'His tomb in the crypt attracts many to Assisi. But in a Holy Year, relics are even better. If we but had the tongue of the Saint, or a lock of his hair, or a fingernail.'

The Bishop had a far-away look in his eyes, and he was shaking his head gently. 'It is a message we are in need of, my dear Supervisor, a message from a great heart that would speak to us across the gap of seven centuries to remind us of The Way.' And here he paused and coughed, for he was a polite man and noticed that Pepino was waiting.

The Supervisor turned also and said, 'Ah yes, my son, what is it that I can do for you?'

Pepino said, 'Please, sir, my donkey Violetta is very sick. The Doctor Bartoli has said he can do nothing more and perhaps she will die. Please, I would like permission to take her into the tomb of Saint Francis and ask him to cure her. He loved all animals, and particularly little donkeys. I am sure he will make her well.'

The Supervisor looked shocked. 'A donkey. In the crypt. However did you come to that idea?'

Pepino explained about Giani and his sick kitten, while the Bishop turned away to hide a smile.

But the Supervisor was not smiling. He asked, 'How did this Giani succeed in smuggling a kitten into the tomb?'

Since it was all over, Pepino saw no reason for not telling, and replied, 'Under his coat, sir.'

The Supervisor made a mental note to warn the

brothers to keep a sharper eye out for small boys or other persons with suspicious-looking lumps under their outer clothing.

'Of course we can have no such goings on,' he said. 'The next thing you know, everyone would be coming, bringing a sick dog, or an ox, or a goat, or even a pig. And then where should we end up? A veritable sty.'

'But, sir,' Pepino pleaded, 'no one need know. We would come and go so very quickly.'

The Supervisor's mind played. There was something touching about the boy – the bullet head, the enormous eyes, the jug-handle ears. And yet, what if he permitted it and the donkey then died, as seemed most likely if Dr Bartoli had said there was no further hope? Word was sure to get about, and the shrine would suffer from it. He wondered what the Bishop was thinking and how *he* would solve the problem.

He equivocated: 'And besides, even if we were to allow it, you would never be able to get your donkey around the turn at the bottom of the stairs. So, you see, it is quite impossible.'

'But there is another entrance,' Pepino said. 'From the old church. It has not been used for a long time, but it could be opened just this once – couldn't it?'

The Supervisor was indignant. 'What are you saying – destroy church property? The entrance has been walled up for over a century, ever since the new crypt was built.'

The Bishop thought he saw a way out and said gently to the boy, 'Why do you not go home and pray to Saint Francis to assist you? If you open your heart to him and have faith, he will surely hear you.'

'But it wouldn't be the same,' Pepino cried, and his voice was shaking with the sobs that wanted to come. 'I must take her where Saint Francis can see her. She isn't like any other old donkey – Violetta has the sweetest smile. She does not smile any more since she has been so ill. But perhaps she would, just once more for Saint Francis. And when he saw it he would not be able to resist her, and he would make her well. I know he would!'

The Supervisor knew his ground now. He said, 'I am sorry, my son, but the answer is no.'

But even through his despair and the bitter tears he shed as he went away, Pepino knew that if Violetta was to live he must not take no for an answer.

'Who is there, then?' Pepino asked of Father Damico later. 'Who is above the Supervisor and my lord the Bishop who might tell them to let me take Violetta into the crypt?'

Father Damico's stomach felt cold as he thought of the dizzying hierarchy between Assisi and Rome. Nevertheless, he explained as best he could, concluding with, 'And at the top is His Holiness, the Pope

himself. Surely his heart would be touched by what has happened if you were able to tell him, for he is a great and good man. But he is busy with important weighty affairs, Pepino, and it would be impossible for him to see you.'

Pepino went back to Niccolo's stable, where he ministered to Violetta, fed and watered her and rubbed her muzzle a hundred times. Then he withdrew his money from the stone jar buried under the straw and counted it. He had almost three hundred lire. A hundred of it he set aside and promised to his friend Giani if he would look after Violetta, while Pepino was gone, as if she were his own. Then he patted her once more, brushed away the tears that had started again at the sight of how thin she was, put on his jacket, and went out on the high road, where, using his thumb as he had learned from Corporal Francis Xavier O'Halloran, he got a lift in a lorry going to Foligno and the main road. He was on his way to Rome to see the Holy Father.

Never had any small boy looked quite so infinitesimal and forlorn as Pepino standing in the boundless and almost deserted, since it was early in the morning, St Peter's Square. Everything towered over him – the massive dome of St Peter's, the obelisk of Caligula, the Bernini colonnades. Everything contrived to make him look pinched and miserable in his bare feet, torn trousers, and ragged jacket. Never was a boy more overpowered, lonely, and frightened, or carried a greater burden of unhappiness in his heart.

For now that he was at last in Rome, the gigantic proportions of the buildings and monuments, their awe and majesty, began to sap his courage, and he seemed to have a glimpse into the utter futility and hopelessness of his mission. And then there would arise in his mind a picture of the sad little donkey who did not smile any more, her heaving flanks and clouded eyes, and who would surely die unless he could find help for her. It was thoughts like these that enabled him finally to cross the piazza and

timidly approach one of the smaller side entrances
to the Vatican.

The Swiss guard, in his slashed red, yellow, and
blue uniform, with his long halberd, looked enormous and forbidding. Nevertheless, Pepino edged
up to him and said, 'Please, will you take me to see
the Pope? I wish to speak to him about my donkey
Violetta, who is very ill and may die unless the Pope
will help me.'

The guard smiled, not unkindly, for he was used
to these ignorant and innocent requests, and the fact
that it came from a dirty, ragged little boy, with eyes
like ink pools and a round head from which the ears
stood out like the handles on a cream jug, made it all
the more harmless. But, nevertheless, he was shaking
his head as he smiled, and then said that His Holiness was a very busy man and could not be seen. And
the guard grounded his halberd with a thud and let
it fall slantwise across the door to show that he meant
business.

Pepino backed away. What good was his precept
in the face of such power and majesty? And yet the
memory of what Corporal O'Halloran had said told
him that he must return to the Vatican yet once
again.

At the side of the piazza he saw an old woman
sitting under an umbrella, selling little bouquets and
nosegays of spring flowers – daffodils and jonquils,

snowdrops and white narcissus, Parma violets and lilies of the valley, vari-coloured carnations, pansies, and tiny sweetheart roses. Some of the people visiting St Peter's liked to place these on the altar of their favourite saint. The flowers were crisp and fresh from the market, and many of them had glistening drops of water still clinging to their petals.

Looking at them made Pepino think of home and Father Damico and what he had said of the love St Francis had for flowers. Father Damico had the gift of making everything he thought and said sound like poetry. And Pepino came to the conclusion that if St Francis, who had been a holy man, had been so fond of flowers, perhaps the Pope, who according to his position was even holier, would love them, too.

For fifty lire he bought a tiny bouquet in which a spray of lilies of the valley rose from a bed of dark violets and small red roses crowded next to yellow pansies all tied about with leaf and feather fern and paper lace.

From a stall where postcards and souvenirs were sold, he begged pencil and paper, and laboriously composed a note:

Dear and most sacred Holy Father: These flowers are for you. Please let me see you and tell you about my donkey Violetta who is dying and they will not let me take her to see Saint Francis so that he may cure her. I

live in the town of Assisi, but I have come all the way
here to see you.

Your loving Pepino.

Thereupon, he returned to the door, placed the
bouquet and the note in the hand of the Swiss guard,
and begged, 'Please take these up to the Pope. I am
sure he will see me when he receives the flowers
and reads what I have written.'

The guard had not expected this. The child and
the flowers had suddenly placed him in a dilemma
from which he could not extricate himself in the
presence of those large and trusting eyes. However,
he was not without experience in handling such mat-
ters. He had only to place a colleague at his post,
go to the Guard Room, throw the flowers and the
note into the wastepaper basket, absent himself for
a sufficient length of time, and then return to tell
the boy that His Holiness thanked him for the gift
of the flowers and regretted that press of important
business made it impossible for him to grant him an
audience.

This little subterfuge the guard put into motion
at once; but when he came to completing the next-
to-last act in it, he found to his amazement that
somehow he could not bring himself to do it. There
was the wastepaper basket, yawning to receive the
offering, but the little nosegay seemed to be glued
to his fingers. How gay, sweet, and cool the flowers

were. What thoughts they brought to his mind of spring in the green valleys of his far-off canton of Luzern. He saw again the snow-capped mountains of his youth, the little gingerbread houses, the grey, soft-eyed cattle grazing in the blossom-carpeted meadows, and he heard the heart-warming tinkling of their bells.

Dazed by what had happened to him, he left the Guard Room and wandered through the corridors, for he did not know where to go or what to do with his burden. He was eventually encountered by a busy little Monsignor, one of the vast army of clerks and secretaries employed in the Vatican, who paused, astonished at the sight of the burly guard helplessly contemplating a tiny posy.

And thus occurred the minor miracle whereby Pepino's plea and offering crossed the boundary in the palace that divided the mundane from the spiritual, the lay from the ecclesiastical.

For to the great relief of the guard, the Monsignor took over the burning articles that he had been unable to relinquish; and this priest they touched, too, as it is the peculiar power of flowers that while they are universal and spread their species over the world, they invoke in each beholder the dearest and most cherished memories.

In this manner, the little bouquet passed on and

upward from hand to hand, pausing briefly in the possession of the clerk of the Apostolic Chamber, the Privy Almoner, the Papal Sacristan, the Master of the Sacred Palaces, the Papal Chamberlain. The dew vanished from the flowers; they began to lose their freshness and to wilt, passing from hand to hand. And yet they retained their magic, the message of love and memories that rendered it impossible for any of these intermediaries to dispose of them.

Eventually, then, they were deposited with the missive that accompanied them on the desk of the man for whom they had been destined. He read the note and then sat there silently contemplating the blossoms. He closed his eyes for a moment, the better to entertain the picture that arose in his mind of himself as a small Roman boy taken on a Sunday into the Alban Hills, where for the first time he saw violets growing wild.

When he opened his eyes at last, he said to his secretary, 'Let the child be brought here. I will see him.'

Thus it was that Pepino at last came into the presence of the Pope, seated at his desk in his office. Perched on the edge of a chair next to him, Pepino told the whole story about Violetta, his need to take her into the tomb of St Francis, about the Supervisor who was preventing him, and all about Father

Damico, too, and the second entrance to the crypt, Violetta's smile, and his love for her – everything, in fact, that was in his heart and that now poured forth to the sympathetic man sitting quietly behind the desk.

And when, at the end of half an hour, he was ushered from the presence, he was quite sure he was the happiest boy in the world. For he had not only the blessing of the Pope, but also, under his jacket, two letters, one addressed to the lay Supervisor of

the Monastery of Assisi and the other to Father Damico. No longer did he feel small and overwhelmed when he stepped out on to the square again past the astonished but delighted Swiss guard. He felt as though he could give one leap and a bound and fly back to his Violetta's side.

Nevertheless, he had to give heed to the more practical side of transportation. He inquired his way to a bus that took him to where the Via Flaminia became a country road stretching to the north, then plied his thumb backed by his eloquent eyes, and before nightfall of that day, with good luck, was home in Assisi.

After a visit to Violetta had assured him that she had been well looked after and at least was no worse than she had been before his departure, Pepino proudly went to Father Damico and presented his letters as he had been instructed to do.

The Father fingered the envelope for the Supervisor and then, with a great surge of warmth and happiness, read the one addressed to himself. He said to Pepino, 'Tomorrow we will take the Supervisor's letter to him. He will summon masons and the old door will be broken down and you will be able to take Violetta into the tomb and pray there for her recovery. The Pope himself has approved it.'

The Pope, of course, had not written the letters

personally. They had been composed with considerable delight and satisfaction by the Cardinal-Secretary, backed by Papal authority, who said in his missive to Father Damico:

Surely the Supervisor must know that in his lifetime the blessed Saint Francis was accompanied to chapel by a little lamb that used to follow him about Assisi. Is an *asinus* any less created by God because his coat is rougher and his ears longer?

And he wrote also of another matter, which Father Damico imparted to Pepino in his own way.

He said, 'Pepino, there is something you must understand before we go to see the Abbot. It is your hope that because of your faith in St Francis he will help you and heal your donkey. But had you thought, perhaps, that he who dearly cared for all of God's creatures might come to love Violetta so greatly that he would wish to have her at his side in Eternity?'

A cold terror gripped Pepino as he listened. He managed to say, 'No, Father, I had not thought –'

The priest continued: 'Will you go to the crypt only to ask, Pepino, or will you also, if necessary, be prepared to give?'

Everything in Pepino cried out against the possibility of losing Violetta, even to someone as beloved as St Francis. Yet when he raised his stricken face and looked into the lustrous eyes of Father Damico,

there was something in their depths that gave him the courage to whisper, 'I will give – if I must. But, oh, I hope he will let her stay with me just a little longer.'

The clink of the stonemason's pick rang again and again through the vaulted chamber of the lower church, where the walled-up door of the passageway leading to the crypt was being removed. Nearby waited the Supervisor and his friend the Bishop, Father Damico, and Pepino, large-eyed, pale, and silent. The boy kept his arms about the neck of Violetta and his face pressed to hers. The little donkey was very shaky on her legs and could barely stand.

The Supervisor watched humbly and impassively while broken bricks and clods of mortar fell as the breach widened and the freed current of air from the passage swirled the plaster dust in clouds. He was a just man for all his weakness, and had invited the Bishop to witness his rebuke.

A portion of the wall proved obstinate. The mason attacked the archway at the side to weaken its support. Then the loosened masonry began to tumble again. A narrow passageway was effected, and through the opening they could see the distant flicker of the candles placed at the altar wherein rested the remains of St Francis.

Pepino stirred towards the opening. Or was it Violetta who had moved nervously, frightened by the unaccustomed place and noises? Father Damico said, 'Wait,' and Pepino held her; but the donkey's uncertain feet slipped on the rubble and then lashed out in panic, striking the side of the archway where it had been weakened. A brick fell out. A crack appeared.

Father Damico leaped and pulled boy and animal out of the way as, with a roar, the side of the arch collapsed, laying bare a piece of the old wall and the hollow behind it before everything vanished in a cloud of dust.

But when the dust settled, the Bishop, his eyes starting from his head, was pointing to something that rested in a niche of the hollow just revealed. It was a small, grey, leaden box. Even from there they could see the year 1226, when St Francis died, engraved on the side, and the large initial 'F.'

The Bishop's breath came out like a sigh. 'Ah, could it be? The legacy of Saint Francis! Fra Leo mentions it. It was hidden away centuries ago, and no one has ever been able to find it since.'

The Supervisor said hoarsely, 'The contents! Let us see what is inside – it may be valuable!'

The Bishop hesitated. 'Perhaps we had best wait. For this is in itself a miracle, this finding.'

But Father Damico, who was a poet and to whom St Francis was a living spirit, cried, 'Open it, I beg of you! All who are here are humble. Surely Heaven's plan has guided us to it.'

The Abbot held the lantern. The mason with his careful, honest workman's hands deftly loosed the bindings and pried the lid of the airtight box. It opened with an ancient creaking of its hinge and revealed what had been placed there more than seven centuries before.

There was a piece of hempen cord, knotted as though, perhaps, once it had been worn about the waist. Caught in the knot, as fresh as though it had grown but yesterday, was a single sprig of wheat. Dried and preserved, there lay, too, the stem and starry flower of a mountain primrose and, next to it, one downy feather from a tiny meadow bird.

Silently the men stared at these objects from the past to try to read their meaning, and Father Damico wept, for to him they brought the vivid figure of the Saint, half-blinded, worn and fragile, the cord knotted at his waist, singing, striding through a field of wheat. The flower might have been the first discovered by him after a winter's snow, and addressed as 'Sister Cowslip,' and praised for her tenderness and beauty. As though he were transported there, Father Damico saw the little field bird fly trustingly to Francis' shoulder and chirrup and nestle there and leave a feather in his hand. His heart was so full he thought he could not bear it.

The Bishop, too, was close to tears as, in his own way, he interpreted what they had found. 'Ah, what could be clearer than the message of the Saint? Poverty, love, and faith. This is his bequest to all of us.'

Pepino said, 'Please, lords and sirs, may Violetta and I go into the crypt now?'

They had forgotten him. Now they started up from their contemplation of the touching relics.

Father Damico cleared the tears from his eyes. The doorway was freed now, and there was room for boy and donkey to pass. 'Ah, yes,' he said. 'Yes, Pepino. You may enter now. And may God go with you.'

The hoofs of the donkey went sharply *clip-clop, clip-clop* on the ancient flagging of the passageway. Pepino did not support her now, but walked beside, hand just resting lightly and lovingly on her neck. His round, cropped head with the outstanding ears was held high, and his shoulders were bravely squared.

And to Father Damico it seemed, as they passed, whether because of the uneven light and the dancing shadows, or because he wished it so, that the ghost, the merest wisp, the barest suspicion of a smile had returned to the mouth of Violetta.

Thus the watchers saw boy and donkey silhouetted against the flickering oil lamps and altar candles of the crypt as they went forward to complete their pilgrimage of faith.